This book belongs to:

....

....

Written by Jillian Harker
Illustrated by Andy Everitt-Stewart

This edition published by Parragon in 2010

Parragon
Queen Street House
4 Queen Street
BATH, BA1 1HE, UK

ISBN 978-1-4054-7156-5
Printed in China

Oakey's Perfect Day

Bath New York Singapore Hong Kong Cologne Delhi Melbourne

Oakey looked out the window. He noticed the lane, winding over the hill and far away.

Suddenly he thought, "I don't want to stay in and play. The world's so big, and I'd like to see more."

Oakey found Mom and said, "I want to go off and explore."

"I have lots to do, so I can't come out with you," Mom said. "But you can go as far as the curve in the lane, across the big field, and then back again. I'll be able to see you."

Mom packed a carrot, an apple, and a sandwich
in Oakey's bag.
"In case you get hungry," she said, smiling.

Oakey skipped off.

Down the lane, Oakey heard Horse grumbling,
"The farmer hasn't brought my food. I'm *so* hungry!"
"You can have this," said Oakey, holding out his carrot.
Horse crunched the carrot noisily.

"Perfect!" he grinned.
"Would you like a ride?"
"I don't have time," explained Oakey.
"I've got the whole world to explore."
And he climbed over the gate.

Halfway across the field, Oakey heard Pig groaning, "Where's the farmer with my food? I'm *really* hungry!"

"Would you like this?" asked Oakey, holding out his apple.

Pig gobbled the apple greedily. "Perfect!" he grinned. "Would you like to see my trick?"

"I don't have time," explained Oakey.
"I've got the whole world to explore."
And he headed toward the pond.

the pond, Oakey heard Duck complaining,
...er's forgotten my bread. I'm *very* hungry!"
...an have mine," said Oakey, holding out
...wich.
... swallowed it swiftly. "Perfect!" she grinned.
... you like a guide on your journey?"

"I know where I'm going," answered Oakey.
"I've got the whole world to explore."
And he wandered on.

Oakey didn't notice the grass getting higher...
and higher.
Suddenly, he couldn't see where he was going.

"I'm lost!" cried Oakey.
"How will I get home?"

"I can see the way," quacked Duck, from above Oakey's head. "Shall I lead you home?"
"Perfect!" Oakey replied.

But the way home seemed very long indeed.
"I'll never get back," sobbed Oakey.

"Cheer up!" said Pig, poking his head through the grass. He turned a cartwheel and fell flat on his nose. "Perfect!" Oakey laughed. "I feel much better now." And he went on.

But before long, Oakey grew tired.
"I can't walk any farther," he sighed.

"Then how about riding on me?" neighed Horse,
appearing as if from nowhere.
"Perfect!" smiled Oakey.

Off they went. Duck flew ahead.
Pig cartwheeled along.
And Horse carried Oakey all the
way home.

Oakey's Mom was waiting.
"Well, was it fun to explore?" she asked.
"Do you think you'd like to see more?"

"I'd like to see more of my new friends," Oakey replied.

"Of course!" smiled Mom. "Let's invite them to lunch."

ROSE COTTAGE

Oakey was as happy as he could be.

"Just perfect!" he said.

The end